HORSE DIARIES

· Black Cloud ·

HORSE DIARIES

#1: Elska

#2: Bell's Star

#3: Koda

#4: Maestoso Petra

#5: Golden Sun

#6: Yatimah

#7: Risky Chance

#8: Black Cloud

HORSE DIARIES

Black Cloud

PATRICIA HERMES

illustrated by ASTRID SHECKELS

RANDOM HOUSE NEW YORK

Text copyright © 2012 by Patricia Hermes
Cover art copyright © 2012 by Ruth Sanderson
Interior illustrations copyright © 2012 by Astrid Sheckels
Photograph credits: © Associated Press (p. 151); © Bob Langrish (p. 148)

All rights reserved. Published in the United States by Random House Children's Books,
a division of Random House, Inc., New York.

Random House and the colophon are registered trademarks of Random House, Inc.

Visit us on the Web! www.randomhouse.com/kids

Educators and librarians, for a variety of teaching tools,
visit us at www.randomhouse.com/teachers

Library of Congress Cataloging-in-Publication Data
Hermes, Patricia.
Black Cloud / Patricia Hermes ; illustrated by Astrid Sheckels. — 1st ed.
p. cm. — (Horse diaries ; 8)
Summary: Despite the dangers, Black Cloud enjoys his life as a
wild mustang colt in 1951 Nevada but when humans round up and
slaughter his herd, he is rescued by a talkative girl named Annie
who gives him a safe and comfortable life, lacking nothing but freedom.
ISBN 978-0-375-86881-8 (trade) — ISBN 978-0-375-96881-5 (lib. bdg.) —
ISBN 978-0-375-89964-5 (ebook)
1. Mustang—Juvenile fiction. [1. Mustang—Fiction. 2. Horses—Fiction.
3. Human-animal relationships—Fiction. 4. Nevada—History—20th century—Fiction.
5. California—History—20th century—Fiction.] I. Sheckels, Astrid, ill. II. Title.
PZ10.3.H466Bl 2012 [Fic]—dc23 2011020784

Printed in the United States of America

10 9 8 7 6 5 4 3 2 1

First Edition

For the cousins:

Lizzie and Mikie and Ben.

And for London.

—P.H.

For my father,

who first drew horses with me.

—A.S.

CONTENTS

"Oh! if people knew what a comfort to horses a light hand is . . ."
—from *Black Beauty*, by Anna Sewell

HORSE DIARIES
· Black Cloud ·

Northern Nevada

Early Spring, 1951

It was spring when I was born. From the moment I opened my eyes and tried gathering myself up onto my wobbly legs, I knew that I was the luckiest colt ever.

Course, I didn't gather myself up fast just

like that. Legs don't do what you want them to do when you've just been born. I lay on the ground awhile, trying to figure out where I was and maybe even what I was. But after resting a bit, I could tell that my first job was to get my legs under me and heave myself up. I tried.

It didn't work real well. I got partway up. And then my legs buckled at the knees, and down I went, so that my belly was flat on the ground. I tried again, and then again. My mama was nearby. She kept nickering at me, *That's good; what a good boy. You're doing just fine.*

Well, not so fine. Down I went again. Hard.

Mama kept standing beside me and saying how well I was doing, and she looked me right in the eye when she said it, so I knew she meant it. After a bit more getting up and falling down, I

was standing. Now I was right up there by my mama, and I could see her and smell her. Just like that, I knew what to do. I buried my nose in her side and began nursing.

Like I said, I was the luckiest colt alive.

Still, it was hard work, and my legs were wobbling, so it was time for a nap. I collapsed on the ground, right where I was, and Mama lay down beside me. I slept really hard and really long, and when I woke I was hungry again. So I nursed some more. And course, that made me tired, too. So after I was done, I slept again.

It took a few more days of nursing and resting and practicing before my legs were any good to me at all. I'd stand. Wobble. Fall over. I'd stand again. Wobble more. And collapse in a heap. One day, I twisted myself up so much, it seemed my legs were wrapped halfway around my neck.

That time, it took all the smarts I had to untuck myself and get to my feet again. But once I did it, I found I could stand. And each day, I stood a little longer. And longer. Soon enough, after a few days, when I reached to my mama to nurse, my legs hardly trembled at all. If they started to wobble after a bit, I just lay down wherever I was and slept.

Mama said I slept real good. Real, real good. She said she'd never seen a horse who could sleep so hard. Sleep was just what I needed, because when I woke up, I had all the energy I wanted to set off running. And oh, how my legs carried me after just a few days, farther and faster.

First, though, before I could run ahead, I had to see where I was going. That's because in those early days, my eyes weren't much better than my legs. Things nearby I could make out just fine, like my mama, but things far away were blurred. Suddenly, though, one morning, when the sun poked its face over the hills, I could make out lots of new things, and my mama told me what they were.

There were trees that waved at me, like they were happy to see me and wanted to say howdy. They were scrubby and skinny, but Mama said they gave shade to us when the sun got hot. There were birds, big ones and little ones, with wings that made them fly high into the sky. The birds could even sit in the treetops! Some of the big ones were awful noisy. But others made sweet little sounds at twilight, so that I fell asleep listening to them.

Mama showed me streams and rocks. I found out that streams moved, and rocks didn't. My mama liked the stream almost as much as I liked her milk. She buried her nose in the water, drinking and drinking. I didn't like the stream, except for splashing in a bit. I even splashed my

mama at times, just to tease her, then turned and fled, in case she got angry. She never did.

Mama told me many things, and she got specially talkative at night when we lay quietly together. One night, she told me she had chosen a name for me—Black Cloud. Because, Mama said, my body was black as night, just like hers. But I also had big patches of light against the dark that looked like clouds. I liked that thought—that clouds fell right out of the night sky and onto me, as though they had chosen me.

I learned from Mama that when she realized it was time for me to be born, she had wandered away from the rest of the herd—even away from my sire, my papa—till she found this perfect place. It was a sweet, soft meadow we were in, tucked low between rocky cliffs that towered above us. It was safe, Mama said, and I mustn't leave it till we were both ready to go together.

Mama also said we were lucky that there were no icy rains pelting us like earlier that spring. Course, I didn't know what rain was yet, but Mama said I'd see soon enough. Meanwhile, we had this quiet place so we could be together for a while, and so Mama could tell me all I needed to know.

I remembered everything she told me, too, storing it all up in my head, and Mama said I was a terrible one for questions. She said she'd never known a colt who was so curious, but she also said I was a quick learner, and smarter than anything. I already knew that, though. Mama said I'd need those smarts when we returned to the high desert. We were mustangs, Mama said, brave and strong and hearty. But there were things out there to watch out for—wolves and rattlesnakes and cougars. And humans.

I didn't know what wolves and rattlesnakes and cougars and humans were. I could tell, though, that Mama's big eyes seemed troubled when she talked about them. I paid little mind. Like I said, I was smart, and I knew Mama could take care of anything. And what she couldn't take care of, I could.

Each day I learned more, storing up knowledge along with my strength. And I began to wonder about things.

One night, I played a game with myself, trying to figure out what I liked best—daytime or nighttime. At first, I thought I liked days the best, because there was sun and I could gallop and play. But then I'd turn around in my mind and think: *I like nighttime the best!* At night, the sky turned black and the trees and cliffs disappeared and other things came in their place. There were those birds that sang me to sleep, and a moon that hung in the sky, lighting up the earth and throwing shadows on the grass. There were stars that poked out of that sky, running right down to earth, and clouds that raced across the dark sky. I thought if I could just gallop to the top of that mountain peak that towered over us, then maybe I could touch the clouds or the stars.

Mama said I couldn't. I didn't really believe her, though I didn't say so. See, Mama wasn't young like me. I bet she couldn't run far and fast like me. So maybe I would try. Someday. Soon. Because, and I told my mama this, someday I would be the biggest, strongest mustang ever. For now, though, for now, I was content to lie beside my mama and think of all I would learn and do the next day, when the stars went away and the sun came up. I slept and I dreamed. And I was happy.

Like I said—I already knew that I was the luckiest colt to ever be born.

2

Predators

It went on that way for I don't know how long—
the big night sky stretching out black above us,
stars blinking. Then day came, and the sun beat
down, and it turned hot, hot, hot. Then night fell
again, the sun dipping below the mountains, and
I got cold and curled up beside my mama for

warmth. One morning, Mama said that soon it would be time to head back to the herd, once I had built up strength in my legs. I was already strong, and I started to tell her that but then stopped.

I had learned that I shouldn't argue with Mama. That was because that morning, I had run too far from her, showing off, she said, and she had whinnied me back and nipped me on the flank. She said I should never leave the safety of the meadow without her, and she made me feel shamed of myself. So I hung my head low, near the ground, so she'd know I was sorry. And for the rest of that day, I stayed real close, because I guessed it was true—that she'd been around awhile. She probably knew a little more than I did.

Still, I knew that one day I would be the

biggest, strongest mustang ever. And each day, I told Mama that.

Then came a night when Mama was fast asleep beside me, and something wakened me.

I lifted my head. I perked my ears forward. Listening. Sniffing the air. The moon was out, round and white, hanging over the hills, lighting up everything in its path. And there, on top of the long crest of the hill on the far side of the meadow, was something that made me wonder. Long-legged creatures. A line of them stretched out along the craggy hilltop.

Horses? The mustang herd my mama had told me about?

I nosed at my mama. *Wake up! Look! The herd has come for us.*

Mama shifted and pushed me off. She didn't

want me to nurse now. Well, I didn't want to nurse, either. I wanted to ask her about those critters on the hilltop. But she just moved away from me in her sleep.

I turned back to the hill and studied those critters some more. They were strung along the rocky hill, and even from that far away, I could see that they had long, long legs, though maybe not as long as mine. There was a pack of them, a family maybe. They held still, staring down at my mama and me. The moon showed them in outline—their pointed ears and heads hung low, tails back. I could tell, even though I'd never seen them before, that they were after something. Had they just come up to meet me? My heart beat hard and fast, the way it did when I was galloping and racing.

This was the herd my mama had told me about! I knew it was. I'd go to them. Maybe my sire, my papa, was among them?

I scrambled to my feet. I was steady enough now, and didn't twist myself all up.

I looked down at Mama. She was still sleeping. She wouldn't be angry at me for leaving. It was just mustangs, the herd, our own kind, so they wouldn't harm me. Quietly, I moved away from Mama, turning toward the rocky cliff. The critters had moved closer by then, coming downhill toward me. One of them seemed to be the leader, slinking low along the ground, the others following. He trotted closer, closer.

I lifted my head and whinnied softly, saying howdy, friendly-like. As they moved to me, I moved toward them, my nose up, sniffing the air.

I trotted all the way across that meadow, till I came to the edge, close by the rocky cliff.

I stopped.

And I knew something then, and my heart went crazy inside me. These weren't horses. They weren't the herd. They smelled bad. Their eyes

glittered in the moonlight, and they moved toward me, holding low to the ground, treachery in their eyes. And hearts. Instinct told me that.

I backed away, my legs getting tangled up again, but I got my footing fast.

I didn't turn tail. Again, my instincts told me

better. I kept facing them, ready to kick out at them, backing away at the same time. But no matter. The lead one leapt from the top of that craggy hill. He flew through the air. Straight at me.

I whirled away and ducked sideways. Not quick enough. In a moment, he was on me, his weight knocking me to the ground. I went down to my knees, squealing in pain.

He sank his teeth into the soft part of my belly.

Rescue

For a moment, the pain was so bad, I couldn't do anything. And then I began to scream. *Mama! Mama!* I struggled back to my feet. Frantic. Terrified.

The critter's jaws were clamped on to my belly, and he hung there, swinging back and forth as I moved. With each movement, the pain tore through me. I tried shaking him off, but his jaws were clamped down hard, and pain surged into my gut.

Then another critter set upon me from behind! He snapped his jaws down on my rear leg. The pain was too much. I collapsed, my knees buckling beneath me.

And then came the sound of fury. Black fur flew in, and my mama was there, swirling and coming on at them like she was four mustangs, not just one. With her jaws, she grabbed the crit-ter hanging on to my belly. She tore him away from me, shaking him loose, and I screamed with pain. Mama flung him hard against a rock, and I heard his head smash.

Then she turned to the one on my leg. She

struck at him with her foreleg. He didn't let go. Mama struck out again. All the time I was trying to shake him off, too, and the pain was screaming through my head and blood was streaming down my leg.

Mama shoved me then. She shoved me hard. She tumbled me over, right onto the ground. I lay there helpless, the critter still clamped tight to my leg. Mama's giant hoof came down on the critter's head. His jaws let loose. Mama didn't stop, though. Furiously, her hooves drove him into the ground, again and again, until he lay still.

She spun around, looking for whom to take on next. But there were no takers. The others had slunk off. The two dead ones lay crushed and broken at our feet.

I trembled as I worked to get my legs under me. I could barely stand, and my heart was beating so hard, surely it would come out of my chest.

Mama nudged at me. *Come,* she said, *come.* She stood close, her shoulder pressed against me, helping support me, while I struggled to my feet. She kept encouraging me, speaking softly, nudging me ahead of her. *Come, my Black Cloud, come. You can do it.*

Night was moving away, and the sky was lightening enough for me to see. Together, Mama and I made our way across the meadow and back to the stand of trees. I was limping and bleeding and didn't know where I hurt the most—leg or belly. Or maybe my heart. I knew I had done something wrong and bad.

I turned and looked back once. The rest of those critters had returned and were feasting on their dead kin!

I started to lie down then, but Mama wouldn't let me. She kept nudging me, circling me, nosing at my wounds. She made little sounds, sad and happy at the same time, and I didn't know what to make of any of it. Finally, she turned her flank to me so I could nurse, and that helped, and when I was done, I collapsed on the ground.

Mama? I said. I didn't have strength to say or ask more.

Wolves, Black Cloud, Mama said. *Wolves.*

Wolves, I thought. Yes, Mama had warned me about wolves. And I was ashamed. I had gone out of the meadow. When I shouldn't. Wolves. And rattlesnakes. And cougars. And humans.

Your wounds aren't deep, Mama said softly. *You'll heal. A few more days and you'll be well.*

I was sure Mama was going to scold and shame me. But she didn't. Not yet, anyway. She just let me sleep.

And sleep was all that I wanted to do.

Home

I was mighty sore for the next few days, but soon enough, my belly healed and the stiffness in my leg wasn't so bad anymore. Once Mama saw me running and leaping about, she said it was time to join up with the herd. She hadn't said a single harsh word about the wolves, and me going off to meet them. Not a word. That was when I realized that Mama understood. And she forgave. She knew I'd learned my lesson. That I knew that I'd almost got myself killed. It wasn't likely I'd do that again.

So, early one morning, after I had nursed and Mama had her fill from the stream, we set off, making our way back to the place where the mustangs roamed free. We trotted along at a good pace, and I was happy to leap ahead and run, though I was careful not to go too far. Like I said, I was smart, and I had learned my lesson.

Only thing was, Mama went on too far and too long. My legs were strong, but I sure got awful tired, and there were times when I lagged behind. But my mama didn't even wait for me, so I had to drag myself along. I got mad at her sometimes, and once, I came close to nipping her on the flank when I finally caught up to her. But I didn't. I was smarter than that.

The sun had come up and gone down and come up again before Mama finally slowed. We were at the top of a ravine, and before us, I could see all the way down to a vast, flat plain. There were pits and holes and rocks between us and the plain. Mama stopped and looked below.

I did, too. And I saw something that I will never, ever, ever forget.

On the floor of the plain were mustangs— horses for as far as I could see. They were all in motion, not galloping or racing along, just moving, flowing the way the stream flowed.

Mama? I said.

Mustangs. Our herd, she answered.

I don't know what I had thought I would see, but I sure hadn't thought of this. I knew they were our kind. I knew for sure the difference between a herd of wolves and a herd of mustangs by now. Still, I was shaking, I was so afraid. There

were so, so many. There was much noise and trampling of feet. And dust. The mustangs were all different sizes and different colors—colts and fillies and mares and stallions—just a flowing, moving mass of mustangs for as far as I could see.

Several young horses, smaller than the rest, were nipping and pushing at one another. Were they playing? Or were they mean and bad? Would they nip and push at me, too?

Suddenly, I didn't feel so sure of myself, and I moved closer to Mama.

Mama? I said again. *Let's go back to the meadow.*

Mama ignored me. Her ears were pricked forward, and I could feel her excitement.

Come, she murmured. *Come.*

She began trotting down the hill, stones and rocks clattering under her hooves. I followed, real unhappy with what I was seeing. One horse, a huge black stallion, was galloping along the edge of the herd, his tail high in the air. As we came to a halt at the base of the hill, he stopped.

He turned and looked at us, his head stretched toward us, ears pressed forward.

Mama lifted her head and whinnied softly, greeting him. The stallion trotted toward us. Closer he came, and closer, till he stopped right in front of us.

I moved behind Mama.

The stallion's ears pricked forward, and his head came up, sniffing, his nostrils widening, breathing in and out hard. He was black with white cloud patches, just like mine, and wild and beautiful and fierce-looking. And very, very scary—the biggest creature I had ever seen, bigger than the wolves, far bigger than my mama.

Mama and the stallion nosed one another for a long time. I could tell that Mama was happy to see him and not at all afraid. She made little nickering sounds and he made sounds back, and I heard my name—*Black Cloud*. They circled one another, nose to tail. Then the enormous stallion turned to face me.

Mama nudged me toward him. *Your sire*, she said. *Courage. All is well.*

I tried to make myself disappear. I closed my eyes. I held my breath. I kept my body still, wishing I could even still my crazy heartbeat.

The stallion—my sire—circled me, not touching me, just circling round and round, sniffing and breathing hard. I could feel the warmth of his breath on my flanks.

I felt Mama's message inside of me: Courage. All is well. I'd always trusted her before, but now I wasn't so sure.

After a moment, the stallion pushed his nose

against my flanks, and I trembled even more, my legs wobbling almost as bad as when I had first been born. He lingered over the wound on my hind leg. Did he know it was a wolf attack? Had Mama told him that I had disobeyed?

Once again, he came full circle till we were face to face. I forced myself to open my eyes.

He was so huge. He lowered his head to mine. I made myself look into his eyes. What I saw made me feel not so afraid. Well, a little bit not so afraid. His eyes were wide and dark, as black as the night. There was strength. And fierceness. But there was something else, too, something that said all was well, just as Mama had said. He looked into my eyes for a long time, and I did my best not to look away. Then he spoke.

Black Cloud, he said. *Black Cloud. It suits you well.*

Instinct told me what to do. I lowered my eyes from his, down to his shoulder, telling him that I knew he was my elder, my sire.

He turned and trotted off, once more to patrol the edge of the herd, while I turned back to Mama.

Come, Mama said. *Come, Black Cloud. We are home.*

The Ways of the Herd

Home.

In the days that followed, I learned a lot about my home and the herd and mustangs. I also learned even more about my mama. Once again, I liked everything that I learned. I discovered that it was the mares who made all the decisions for the herd—and that my mama was the lead mare! Mama didn't just tell *me* what to do. She told the entire herd what to do. There were many different family groups in the herd, but they all followed my mama.

Stallions were different. They didn't lead. They did other things, like patrol the herd for predators. I noticed something else, too—they fought a lot among themselves, even my sire. They didn't pick on the young horses or the mares. They fought only with one another, or sometimes with a half-grown stallion, which seemed awful silly to me. It was as though they all wanted to control certain families or mares, showing off, I always thought.

My mama didn't bother with the stallions much. She had more important things to do.

When she said it was time to move, the herd moved, flowing in long, long lines behind her. When she said we should stop and rest awhile, we stopped. And if Mama sensed predators, she held back while the stallions chased or fought the wolves or cougars.

In our herd, there were lots and lots of young colts and fillies who had been born that spring, some even younger than me. After I became less scared, I joined them, especially the ones in my own family group. We banded together and played. I realized now that what I had seen the first day was just them at play. Sometimes, we cavorted and leapt, racing one another, but never out of sight of our mamas. Sometimes, we even fought, just play-fighting, though, not trying to hurt one another.

Omar, one of the colts in our family group, showed me how to crow-hop, leaping and tumbling about. I made many friends among the colts and fillies, but I liked Omar best because he was the friendliest and most fun for play. We

played until we were so tired we happily rested
when our mamas said it was time for sleep.

Sometimes, one of the older mares came and
circled us younger ones, nosing us back into the
herd if we wandered too far. It was then that I

stopped being afraid of the bigger mares, because I knew they were looking out for us. One day, Artis, an older mare in our family, punished me. She nipped at me, warning me that I was playing too rough with her filly, Abril. I held my nose close to the ground, telling her I hadn't meant to hurt her filly. I wasn't a troublemaker, I was telling her, just careless sometimes. And besides, I really liked Abril.

There was a real troublemaker among us, however, and it was the only thing about the herd and our family group that I didn't like. He was a colt, also, but older than I, a yearling. His name was Sota. I soon discovered that it would be a good idea to stay away from Sota. It turned out that wasn't so easy, though.

One day, while I was playing with Omar, Sota snuck up on me from behind. With no warning, he kicked out at me. It was a sharp, deep kick, and he caught me right in the leg where the wolf had latched on.

I yelped and whirled around, dizzy with pain. I knew it was Sota. But he had moseyed away and begun quietly grazing, as though he hadn't done anything at all.

Another time, he raced right up and nipped me on the flank. I didn't fight back. I didn't even try. I knew I couldn't win a fight with him. He was much bigger than me.

And another time, Sota kicked Omar, and Omar tried kicking back. But like me, Omar was too little to really hurt this bully.

And then, one morning, Sota attacked Abril, the pretty filly in our group. Sota clamped his teeth tightly on Abril's neck and bit down.

Abril spun around and tumbled to her knees.

I watched as she struggled to her feet, injured and bleeding, one ear torn. She limped off, squealing, looking for her mama, Artis. I knew how badly she must hurt. I hadn't forgotten how it felt when the wolves attacked. But this attack wasn't a wolf—this was one of our own kind! It made me angry. But even more, it scared me. I hadn't known that our own kind could be vicious.

So, just as Abril did, I ran for my mama. I wasn't hurt. But I was plenty scared. I stayed with my mama for many moons. I didn't tell Mama why I was clinging to her. I was being cowardly and I knew it, and I was afraid she'd scold me. I knew a mustang should be strong. I'd be strong soon, I was sure of it. I could tell how fast I was growing, and I could feel my strength. My legs didn't wobble at all any longer, not even when I was tired out from playing and running.

Someday soon, I would fight Sota off, just the way my mama had fought off the wolves. I didn't think I'd kill Sota, even if I could. But I would sure show him that he had to behave.

At least, that was what I told myself. I had told my mama I'd be the biggest, bravest mustang ever. Now I was older—and still scared. The entire time I stayed close to my mama, I knew I wasn't big or brave. I was a coward.

And I didn't like the feeling at all.

6

Ousting a Troublemaker

Seasons shifted. Nights became colder, and the days not so hot. And then snow came and winds blew, and then, just as suddenly, winds blew the snow away, and small shoots of green appeared, and it was spring again. It had been a whole year since I was born. I was a yearling. And I was still scared and timid. But as spring blossomed and green grass waved over the plains, I also became bored with myself. I was tired of being a scared little colt. Besides, I missed my friends. I could feel myself getting stronger every day, and so, after all that time of clinging close to my mama, I decided I'd go back. I was maturing, I could feel it. I even saw younger colts admiring me—how fast I could run, how nimble I was. And I was learning the way of the herd. I learned a lot from my mama. I decided that if Sota bothered me, I was strong enough now to fight him off. I had learned play-fighting with the other colts, but we never hurt one another. It scared me to think that I might have to fight Sota for real. But I would do it. I knew I could.

I thought I could.

And then, on the very morning that I decided to be brave again and join my friends, Mama did something that made my heart leap and be happy.

I was with my friends, playing beside Omar. Sota was behind me—I could sense and smell him, but he hadn't bothered me. Yet. Suddenly, Mama appeared.

She shouldered me aside. She faced Sota. She squared her shoulders at him, charged him, and knocked him to the ground.

Because I'd been playing with Omar, I hadn't seen what Sota had done. But knowing him, he'd been bullying somebody. I didn't know if Mama was defending me. Maybe she'd known that whole long winter that Sota had been ter-rifying me, and that was why she had come along that morning. Or else maybe she'd just had enough of Sota, too.

At any rate, once Sota got back to his feet, Mama went to work on him. Except for that one shove that knocked him down, she didn't fight him, kicking and biting him the way stallions do. Instead, she did what all mares do—she circled out toward him, squaring her body up to his, fixing him with her eyes. She was ordering him out of the herd! She kept moving toward him, ordering him farther and farther away until she had forced him to retreat to a rocky ledge, all by himself. Then Mama returned to the herd.

Sota stayed out on that ledge. But not for long. Soon he began to inch his way closer, little by little.

Again, Mama turned and faced him. This

time, she drove him even farther away, so far that he was on the other side of the ridge.

That sure made me feel relieved. Still, I knew Sota pretty well by now. I knew that he didn't intend to stay out, no matter what Mama did. But Mama was smarter than Sota. Each time he crept back, she forced him farther away. Finally, she moved him so far out, I could barely see him. He was no more than a dot on the horizon.

It went on that way all day. And then, in the late afternoon, Sota got sneaky. He disappeared from the horizon. For a long time he was gone— and then I spotted him. He had made a wide circle about the herd. He had circled all the way round to the other side.

Omar and I were side by side, playing and

crow-hopping some with Abril, but watching this all the time.

He thinks he's clever, I said.

Won't fool your mama, Abril answered.

He's trying, though, Omar said.

Won't work! I said.

I was right. Mama caught up with Sota. She turned her body and fixed her eyes on him, so fierce that he had to retreat. She drove him right back out beyond the ridge. I thought he was lucky that she didn't nip him or kick at him. But that wasn't the way of mares. Still, what she was doing to him was worse. Omar and I understood that. Abril understood it, too. If Mama didn't allow Sota back in by dark, he'd be dead by morning. Nighttime was death time for lone creatures. Up on that ridge alone, he'd be set upon by wolves or cougars the minute the sun went down.

We had met up with cougars before, fast and ugly cats who circled us, longing for the foal who might wander from the herd. I had seen a stallion fight off a cougar one night. The stallion had killed the cougar with his swift heels. But the stallion had been terribly wounded. He limped and bled and couldn't keep up and dropped back out of the herd the next day. I knew that stallion was dead by now. And if Mama didn't let Sota back in, that would be his fate, too.

I couldn't take my eyes off Mama. And Sota. I had known my mama was strong. I hadn't realized how fierce she could be. Would she really let him die out there?

The sun was low in the sky when things began to change. It wasn't Mama who changed. It was Sota. He seemed to decide that Mama had won and it would be smart to apologize before dark. He stayed away from the herd as ordered, far away on the ridge, no longer inching in. But as he trotted along, he bent his neck. He let his head hang low, really low, his eyes fixed on the ground, not looking up. He walked along the ridge for a long time that way. He kept his nose so low to the ground that I knew he had to be breathing in dirt and dust.

It was clear what he was doing. With his head low like that, he was apologizing.

Mama ignored him.

Sota tried harder. He began making chewing motions with his mouth, his tongue sliding in and out, his nose almost on the ground. He was show-ing that if he was eating, he wasn't a threat. He was just a small, innocent horse. *I'm sorry*, he was saying. *I know you're in charge. I won't do it again.*

I sure hoped he meant it.

I looked toward my mama.

She didn't relent, though. Not yet. She kept him out until the sun was almost below the hills. Only a faint light was left in the sky when finally, finally, Mama relented. She turned her shoulders slightly. She signaled with her eyes.

Sota lifted his head. Slowly, quietly, he moved toward the herd. It took a while, because he had been forced so far away. And when he trotted in among us, he was as quiet and docile as a newborn colt.

He came to Mama's side. They stood together

for a bit. I don't know what they said between them, all of it with their eyes, their bodies. But surely, Sota was saying sorry.

After a while, Mama began to groom him. She licked and licked him. She gave him a really, really good grooming, while he stood still, docile, comfortable.

It was the way of the mares—she was telling him that he was forgiven.

The rest of us youngsters had watched this all day. I think we were all happy that Sota had been punished. But I was also glad that he had been allowed back in. He was a terrible bully. But I hated to think of him dead.

I knew one thing for certain, though: Mama would keep a good eye on him from now on. I was pretty sure that Sota hadn't completely changed. But I also knew this: Sota knew what would happen if he tried bullying again.

After that day, things were better in the herd, better for us young ones who wanted to play free and safe from mean Sota. And better for everyone. There was no room in our family group, or anywhere in the herd, for a trouble-maker. And Mama had just made that clear.

I was proud of my mama, proud of the way she had protected me—and all of us. With Mama in charge, all was well. Just as she had said.

Restless and Worried

Spring edged into summer, and once more, the days became hot. The ground was dry, with little water, and Mama kept us all on the move, looking for better grazing and better water holes. But I began to notice something. Mama and the other mares seemed anxious, worried, and restless. Even at night, Mama didn't sleep much.

One night I woke, wanting to nuzzle close to her. Now that I was more than a year old, I was no longer nursing. Yet I liked being close. But that night when I awoke, she was gone.

I scrambled to my feet. Where was she? The other mares were circling, worrying with one another, restless, their ears laid back. But no Mama.

My heart began that awful, fearsome pounding. I remembered what Mama had warned me about back in the peaceful days of the meadow— wolves and rattlesnakes and cougars and humans. Rattlesnakes I had seen. They were everywhere, and Mama had taught me ways to watch out for their holes. She told me how to avoid them when they came out to warm themselves on rocks in the early-morning sun, and how to leap aside if one struck out. But rattlesnakes disappeared at night.

Had Mama sniffed out a cougar circling us? Was that where she had gone? Or had she been snatched by a cougar? Or a wolf? My heart was pounding so hard I was sure Mama could hear it—wherever she was.

I nosed my way into the group of mares. They paid no attention to me. I was too young to be bothered with. Immature. I could tell by their posture. Their eyes were focused somewhere else. I was too ashamed to ask, *Where's my mama?* It was foolish and childish. Mustangs are brave. And strong.

And sometimes, a little scared.

And then, while I stood fretting, trying to decide whether to speak up or not, Mama appeared. She trotted up silently, melting into the group of mares as smooth as a black shadow.

I nudged closer to her.

Mama? I asked. Is it wolves?

Mama didn't answer. She bent with the mares, nickering and talking.

I waited awhile. A long while.

Mama? I asked again.

Still, Mama didn't answer. She turned her rump toward me, facing the mares. For a long time, she ignored me, whinnying with the older mares, all of them circling and worried and anxious. I stayed with them awhile, although

Mama was acting as if I hadn't even been born to her.

Finally, I went away and lay down alone. I would be brave. I could be brave. Couldn't I?

I was almost asleep when Mama came and lay beside me.

I lifted my head. *Mama?*

Humans, Mama said.

Humans?

They have only two legs. So they latch on to the back of a horse.

To kill us, Mama?

Sometimes. Sometimes worse, Mama said.

Worse than being killed?

They capture us, Mama said. *We can't run free.*

I was quiet awhile, thinking about that.

Mama, I said finally, *if they have just two legs, surely we can outrun them.*

They come from the sky, Mama said. *On wings. Airplanes, the old mares call them.*

Wings? Like birds? I asked.

Like birds, Mama said.

Oh, Mama! I said. *We're not afraid of birds!*

Mama got to her feet. She trotted over to the mares, who were still standing and circling. I felt bad then. I knew I had made Mama mad. She always thought I was too much of a know-it-all. And maybe I was. Sometimes. But it didn't make much sense to me.

Anyway, I didn't ask anything else that night, or for many nights to come.

But as the mares became more restless and

worried, I worried, too. *Courage,* my mama had said when we'd returned to the herd. *All is well.*

It was clear, though, from the way Mama and the other mares continued to circle and sniff and worry together that all was not well.

Even we youngsters began to feel all itchy and anxious, ready to strike out at one another, kind of mean-feeling. Our play became less play and more real. I think we were all as nervous and skittish as the mares, waiting for something that we could sense was coming—something that was worse than an attack by wolves.

Humans!

Still, for a long time, all was peaceful. Summer was a sweet time for us mustangs, with plenty of grazing. In our herd, tempers seemed to calm some. Sota had decided to be less of a bully, and Omar and I were big enough to play at real fighting—though not the kind where we hurt one another. Calm descended over us as the summer went on, even though some mares, especially my mama, continued to be restless.

After a while, cooler weather again settled in. Mama gave the signal that it was time to move on, to look for more lush grazing. And so, one morning, we filled up at the water hole, getting ready to move on, the younger ones splashing one another. I had sort of outgrown my silliness, but I did enjoy sneaking up on Sota and Omar—and even my mama—and splashing them. I snuck up on Abril, too. I kind of liked her.

There were different family groups in our herd, and each waited its turn while the others drank. The sun had just lifted itself over the hills, spilling its light on the desert floor. I was splashing in the water with Omar.

I had my nose almost underwater when the air was jarred by a tremendous sound. The water trembled and moved in waves. I raised my head. We all raised our heads.

Overhead was a bird—an enormous bird. It was dark, and its wings were spread wide, casting a huge shadow. It was bigger than an eagle, bigger than a stallion, even. It brought a howling wind with it, swirling dust all around, dust and dirt that almost blinded us. All of us at the water hole backed out, turning this way and that. We circled wildly, none of us knowing what to do or how to escape.

What was this creature?

And then I remembered Mama. *Humans. They come from the sky. On wings. Airplanes.*

There was no time to think. There was no time to look for Mama. But it was clear that she had given a signal. The herd gathered itself together. As if we were all one horse, we took off, galloping across the desert floor, following Mama's lead.

We ran hard, scattering and sometimes falling, panic forcing us on, right behind Mama. The winged human followed. It stayed with us, right above, right behind, and the noise was terrifying. It didn't settle on us like an eagle with its talons. It just pushed us forward, forward—we didn't know where. Or why.

I couldn't find my mama, and Omar had lost his mama, too.

We stayed close to one another, galloping

along. Omar's eyes were wide and wild, and I knew mine were the same. My heart was pounding with the kind of fear I hadn't felt since the night with

the wolves. And then, as we ran, Sota appeared, galloping beside us.

I moved toward him, warning him not to try any of his bullying tricks. He backed off, saying he understood. I had become bigger and stronger, and he knew it. Still, I knew I'd be no match for him if he chose to attack.

Anyway, we were all so panicked, there was no chance for fighting. All our efforts were spent trying to escape the huge, dark, terrifying human above.

Once, Mama tried to make a shift. The horses in front began to lean into a turn, meaning that Mama wanted us to go back in the direction we had come from. We couldn't turn, though. The human dropped down till it was almost on top of us, blocking our way.

Mama shifted again, and again the herd moved forward, following her lead. The human continued to hover over us, pushing us on, not allowing us to rest, even for a moment. It didn't allow us to graze, either. Or to drink. I thought that I would die of thirst. Once, when the entire herd slowed a moment, the monster human swooped lower, lower, till the noise of its wings was deafening and the wind it brought raised bigger clouds of dust and whipped my mane all about.

I began tripping and stumbling from exhaustion. My lungs ached for air, my chest hurt, and my throat was parched. Omar fell behind. Even Sota showed signs of losing strength.

Omar stopped altogether. He fell back to the side, the herd sweeping on past him.

Omar! Omar! I called to him, urging him on. *Cougars. Wolves. Come!*

Omar staggered a few steps forward. He collapsed on the ground, his knees giving way beneath him.

We couldn't wait. I dared not wait.

Sota circled round. He nipped Omar's flank.

I was too weary to do battle with Sota. But then I realized: Omar had risen to his feet. Sota had bullied him, all right. Bullied him up and onto his feet!

Omar returned to trot along beside me, his breathing labored, his body soaked in sweat. We were all almost dropping from exhaustion and thirst. But we went on. And on. And on.

I faltered, too. How could I go on? I couldn't. Many of our herd had already dropped, falling to the dusty earth, dead before they even hit the ground.

I slowed. I could barely trot. My eyes blurred and I stumbled. I fell to my knees, gasping, longing for water. And then that Sota, he came from nowhere and he nosed me hard. *Come! Come! You can't give up. We can outrun him, we can! You can!*

I thought of Mama. I had promised her I would be the strongest mustang ever. I struggled to my feet.

On we went. We had begun running just as the sun had come up above the horizon. Midday came, and the sun hung overhead, and still we ran. The sun slipped lower in the sky, and that human hung over us, pushing us on. We ran— Omar on one side of me, barely able to stand,

and Sota on the other, limping, but urging us on. Exhausted, we ran into the setting of the sun, trying to escape the thing that hovered over us. The thing that was worse than wolves or cougars.

The thing that was worse than death.

Trapped

It was nearly completely dark when the winged human let up on us. One moment it was bearing down on us; the next moment, it was gone. It disappeared from the sky, just as quickly as it had come.

The herd stopped running as soon as the

winged creature disappeared. We dropped down, exhausted, though I could see in the distance that some mares still moved slowly ahead, as though their legs didn't know how to stop.

We were in a field of stubby grasses and shrubs, with just one small water hole. Every horse, every horse that was still alive, crept to the water hole. I was so tired, I could barely stand and drink. But I let my nose sink into the water. I drank. The water tasted foul, and after just a few moments, I simply held my head under-water, cooling myself. Beside me, a mare fell. She toppled right into the water. I could see that she was dead.

I rested for a little time, flat on the ground, my legs stretched out, lifting my head to look around for my mama, for my friends. On all sides, as far and as high as I could see, were cliffs and mountains—a box canyon. We had been forced into a tight box canyon. Was there no way forward? Was that why the human bird allowed us to stop? He would keep us from going back. I was sure of that, sure that he would return with daylight.

There was another wall that ran alongside us, something I had never seen before. It was a wall of trees, trees with no branches or leaves, trees as high as my shoulders.

Fences, I heard an old mare mutter.

After a while, I forced myself to my feet, my legs trembling and achingly sore.

Mama?

I moved slowly through the herd, looking. I passed many family groups, but not my own.

No Sota, no Omar, no Abril, no Abril's mama, none of the colts and fillies. Had they fallen? Were they all dead? I was hungry and thirsty, but mostly afraid. I so much needed my mama.

I kept moving on, so tired I could barely lift my legs.

And then, at last, up ahead, I saw her. My mama! She was with other mares, at the very front of the pack. She was leading. Still leading. Moving slowly ahead, her head drooping, but weaving back and forth as though looking for a way out. It was clear that even though she was still leading, she could hardly stand. Her whole body drooped, and she was soaked in sweat.

I summoned my energy. *Mama!* I cried.

She turned her head slowly, painfully. She whinnied me to her.

I could see that she was exhausted, her beautiful coat dark with sweat. And blood! She was dark with blood! It poured from both of her front legs and from her neck. Her flesh hung in strips, her bones showing underneath.

Mama! I cried again. *Cougars? Wolves?*

Mama didn't answer. She just waited for me to reach her.

I did. I nuzzled close. *Mama?*

And then, on the far side of the fence, came a human. It had no wings, but I knew it was human. It had just two legs. And it sat atop a horse, just as Mama had warned me about. It was a small female human, and she was with another female, also atop a horse.

The small human cried out. "Mama!" she cried. "Mama!"

I knew that word—I thought I knew that word. But then she cried more, sounds tumbling out, things that meant nothing.

The horse that she rode moved closer to the

fence. *The child's called Annie, the horse said. She'll help you.*

Help me? She's clamped on your back! I cried. *She's clinging like a cougar. She'll kill you, too.*

Not so, fool mustang! the horse said. *She saved me.*

Sounds kept pouring out of the small human, but they made no sense. The horse—he called himself Clay, Big Clay, like he was important or something—he explained some as she talked. But he made no more sense than the child did. Nothing did but that we were trapped and my mama was bleeding to death.

"Oh, no, look!" the small human cried. "Oh, Mama, that mare is bleeding! Look at her!"

They turned to my mama. Clay turned to me.

Barbed wire, Big Clay said. *She the lead mare?*

She's my mama!

Big Clay hung his head.

"Oh, Mama! What can we do for her?" the young one asked.

"Nothing right now, Annie. Nothing," the bigger female said. "She's wild. She won't let us near her."

"But she'll bleed to death!"

"Maybe. Maybe not, Annie," the other female said. "It's almost dark. We can't do anything, at least till daylight. Let's go home to Papa. We'll tackle Jake and the rest in the morning and see which of these poor creatures we can save."

All this talk and more, Big Clay explained to me. Still, none of it made any sense at all. And even if it did, how could I believe him? Trust a horse with a *human* on his back?

"We'll do what we can in the morning," the mama said. "Now look! Look at the mare. There's her colt."

They both turned to me.

"Oh, Mama!" Annie said. "He's so beautiful. Black and white like someone dropped patches of snow on him."

Clouds. But I didn't say it, not even to Clay. *Clouds.*

I nuzzled up to my mama. Mama leaned into me, as though she had forgotten that I no longer suckled from her.

Mama? I cried.

Mama's legs began to fold beneath her. She went down on her knees and then rolled to her side. I could see that she was trying to allow me to nurse, that she had forgotten. I was too old to nurse now. She had forgotten.

Mama?

There's no way out, Mama said.

Oh, Mama! I said.

Black Cloud, she said softly.

She fixed her eyes on mine. And then, slowly, the light went out of them.

Mama. My mama was dead.

10

The Humans Return

I lay beside Mama all night, nuzzling close to her. She was cold, and I tried my best to warm her.

But in the morning, she was still dead.

With the sun rising over the mountains, the humans came back, just as I'd known they would.

They didn't come on wings. They came on horses, clinging to the backs of horses! And they rode right in among us. They drove their horses cruelly, hard and fast. I had thought yesterday that I couldn't have been more frightened. I was frightened today. But more than that, I was wild with fury. My mama was dead! The humans had killed her.

The men began circling horse after horse, one after the other. They threw a thick snake-like thing over the head of each horse, forcing the horse to halt. Most horses tried to fight back, kicking and biting and bucking. But we were exhausted. Even the stallions weren't able to fight. I saw Abril's sire fall and saw Abril leap to help him. But the men swatted her aside, and her sire fell hard, his knees buckling under him.

I looked for my sire, but didn't see him. I knew he was among us somewhere. Did he know Mama was dead?

Once the humans had a horse under control, they grabbed the horse's head. Using a sharp, pointy thing, the humans clamped shut the nostrils of each horse! Some horses sank to their knees immediately. Others remained standing, but they couldn't flee. They were barely able to breathe.

And then they turned on Abril, one on each side! I flew in among them, kicking and biting. Too late. She was small and delicate, and in an instant, they had her on the ground. They clamped her nostrils, closing off her breath.

The men on horseback fled as I stomped into their midst. I tried to get Abril to speak to me, but she didn't, she couldn't. Her pretty ears were laid back, and I knew she was angry and scared, but with the clamps, there was hardly enough air for her to breathe. There was no air left for talking. But her eyes told me. She was frightened. Near to death. She knew it.

I didn't see Sota or Omar anywhere, but I knew that if they weren't dead already they'd fight back. They would.

Each time a horse was encircled, I fled, but I turned, ready to face the humans, ready to fight, bite, and kick. They would not tie me down. I would die. But I would kill them, too, as many as I could.

The men went on. Horse after horse, stallions and mares and colts and fillies, all were hunted down and their nostrils clamped shut.

Each time they came close to me, I circled farther away, bucking and showing them my teeth. But my circling took me away from my mama, and I kept returning to her. I knew she was dead. But I couldn't leave her.

And then there was movement on the far side of the fence. It was the small female, Annie, atop Clay, along with her mama on a horse and a male atop a horse, too.

All three horses seemed well cared for—but they all had humans clinging to their backs!

Clay moved closer to the fence.

Annie's going to help you, he said. *Her mama and papa, too. They'll free you.*

Free! I said. *Free?*

Free. They'll buy your freedom. They bought mine.

You're not free! I said. *You have a human on your back!*

Clay turned away.

Annie began making sounds then, talking, and again, I couldn't understand what she said.

I nickered at Big Clay, and he turned back to me.

I been with them a long time, Clay said. *Since I was real young, younger than you, not even a yearling. I understand them. And so will you someday. So listen to me.*

Listen to a *captured* mustang who'd let humans on his back? Telling me I'd understand humans someday? But what else could I do but listen? Nothing. So as the humans talked, I listened to Clay, my heart thundering with hatred. And fear.

Annie turned to me. "That poor colt!" she said. "His mother is dead. Oh, Papa, can we rescue him?"

"That's what we're here for," the papa said. "If you want, we'll try to get him, along with any others we can. We're going to have a fight on our hands, though. Jake and his clan paid for the plane and corralled them. They own the horses now."

"Own them? Hunted them down, you mean!" Annie said.

"Let's hurry!" the mama said. "We'll buy or wheedle freedom for some of these poor creatures at least."

"Nick," the papa said. "He's the one to see. I'm afraid he's poisoned the water hole, too. See how docile and weak they are?"

The papa turned his horse. "Annie?" he said. "Come along."

"No!" Annie said. "I'm staying here with this colt. I won't let those men near him."

The papa looked at me. He looked at Annie. Big Clay turned to me, too. I reared up on my hind legs, baring my teeth.

Settle down, fool mustang! Clay muttered at me.

I settled down, but hatred still raged inside me.

"Okay," the papa said to Annie. "You can stay. But just *talk* to the men if they come near. Scream and yell if you have to, and Mama or I will come back. But don't get in their way. These men are as dangerous as the mustangs themselves. And don't do anything foolish with that colt, either. Remember, he's wild."

"I'll remember, Papa," Annie said.

And the papa and mama turned and rode off. Leaving me with no one but Big Clay and Annie.

A two-legged human atop the back of a captured mustang.

Annie

I must have let down my guard. I'd been listening to Annie and her mama and papa and eyeing Clay, wondering what he really meant and what he really knew and how he could bear to have a human on his back. By the time I noticed and whirled around, two men atop two huge horses were fast approaching.

They thundered right up to me, one on either side.

"This here's a wild one, Bud!" one of the men yelled. "And mean. Careful."

"Jake!" the other yelled back. "Watch it! He's moving toward you. You got the tongs?"

"Wire and tongs!" Jake answered.

And that was when the small human did something that startled—and terrified—me. She leapt from the top of that horse, Clay. She vaulted over the fence and stood right beside me. I backed up, rearing and turning wildly.

"Are you out of your mind, girl?" Jake shouted. "That's a wild mustang there. Get out of here and over that fence. You'll get yourself killed."

The child didn't move. She faced the men on horseback. "Go away!" she screamed.

Jake and Bud pulled up on their horses, the horses dancing and prancing a little as they backed away.

"Okay, Wild Horse Annie," Jake said. "You made your point. You want to save the horses. We got it. You're a sweet little girl but totally naive. Nice try, but all your talk and all your laws don't matter one hoot to us. Now just get out of our way. Let Bud and me do our job, and everything will be just fine."

Annie stepped sideways, closer to me. I reared up again, my hooves near her head.

Big Clay snorted and stamped on the other side of the fence. *Stop it! Fool!*

"He's going to slam those hooves down on your head!" Jake shouted. "One kick and you'll be dead. Now go! Out of here. Are you stupid or something?"

"No!" Annie said. "Leave this colt alone. You're going to kill them all, aren't you?"

"Sure are," Jake said. "They're eating up our range land, leaving nothing for decent ranchers like us. They'll be crows' bait in a few hours. Now get back on your horse and get out of here, Annie. You're getting to be a real pest. You and your papa and mama and the rest of your kind. I'm going to have to shoot that horse if you don't move before he kills you!"

I had backed up some, snorting and stamping again. She was trying to save me. Big Clay had said so. But she was a human. And I hated her.

"Annie?" Jake said, moving closer. "Out of my way."

"No," Annie said.

"Fine, then," Jake said.

"Okay with me, too," Bud said. Together, they turned their horses and began to trot slowly away.

"We'll be back for that colt!" Jake yelled. "And since he'll have killed you in the meantime, we'll tell your mama and papa where to come to pick up your body."

I looked at Annie. I hated her as I hated the wolves and cougars. She was human. Humans had led us into this trap. And killed my mama. I would smash her head, just as my mama had smashed those wolves.

I reared above her, ready to strike down hard with my hooves.

And then Annie did something amazingly stupid. She sat down. She sat on the ground right in front of me. She sat there, looking at the earth, her eyes turned down.

I lowered my hooves. I backed up. I was ready to fight. But I was confused, too. I circled a bit.

Slowly, Annie turned her body slightly away from me. She didn't meet my eyes. She didn't look at me. She just sat there.

This strange creature with just two legs was talking to me. In horse talk. With her down-turned eyes. With her body. She was trying to tell me something. That she was trying to free me? That she wouldn't harm me? She was talking to me just like my mama spoke to us young colts—teaching us, prodding us, forgiving us. Was Annie telling me not to be afraid of her? That Clay was telling the truth? That she was a good human?

There were no good humans.

I could have killed her, pounded her into the earth, just as my mama had done to the wolves.

I didn't.

12

A Real Know-It-All

The mad stampede of horses, the squalling and screaming went on, but far from us now. The men had corralled the horses into a distant corner, where they were shoving them into a chute of some kind. They even hauled my mama's body away from me. It was just Annie and me. Alone.

And Clay, his tail and ears twitching, nervous as a cougar, stamping and circling on the far side of the fence.

Annie stayed on the ground, not making a sound. She didn't raise her eyes to me. She kept her body slightly turned. She was talking to me in horse talk. By her posture, by her down-turned eyes, she was saying that she wasn't a threat. She was telling me that she wasn't a predator.

But she was. All humans were. Weren't they?

After a while, I came close to her. She was so still, she might have been dead. I didn't touch her. I didn't hurt her. I didn't know why.

After a long, long time, Annie rose to her feet. She didn't look back at me. She walked slowly away. She climbed the fence. She got atop Clay. He nickered, and I knew he was telling her he was relieved. She stayed right there, watching me, both of them watching me, ready to chase away the men, should they come back.

The sun was high overhead by the time all the horses were gone. They had been hauled out of the enclosure. Dead ones, live ones, they were all gone. I hadn't seen Omar, nor Sota, nor my sire. But they were gone.

All of them. Dead. I knew that.

I was the only one left.

Me. And Annie, on the other side of the fence, atop Clay. And then, after a little while, Annie and Big Clay left as well.

I waited for what would happen next. I was too frightened to lie down and rest, and just about starved. There was no grazing left in this awful place, and the water was foul. I thought of trying to leap the fence, but it was too high. And I was so weak.

The day wore on, and just as sunset arrived, so did Annie and her papa, both of them still astride their horses. They stopped beside the fence, where they had talked to me that morning.

Annie called out to me, her voice high with excitement.

She says you're coming to the ranch. With us, Clay said.

I moved toward them. Hesitant. I was so hungry, so thirsty. Did I smell food?

"Okay, big boy," the papa said. "We got something here for you. And then we're going to take you to a nice, safe place."

He lowered something over the fence.

Drink, Big Clay said. *It's water. Good, clear water.*

The papa helped Annie lower something else over the fence to me.

I know you ain't tasted it before, but it's good, Big Clay said. *There are oats mixed in. You'll feel better real soon.*

I stuck my nose in and sniffed. It smelled fine, and I began gobbling it, then drinking, then eating, then drinking some more. I didn't know if I could ever get full again.

Both humans sat atop their horses, watching me. I was glad that they stayed on the far side of the fence. I don't know what I would have done had they dropped down beside me. I was mad at them, but really mad at Clay more than at the humans. How could he hold still like that with a human on his back? How could he act like it was all right?

"I'll go get the truck," Annie's papa said after a time. "There's bound to be some struggle with him, so I'll get help. I'll be back soon as I can. And, Annie?"

"What, Papa?"

"Don't do anything foolish."

"I won't, Papa," Annie answered.

The papa left. Annie stayed. After a while, Annie got off Big Clay and climbed atop the fence. She sat there, swinging those two legs back and forth. I wondered if that was the foolish thing she wasn't supposed to do.

The child began pouring out sounds, things that meant nothing, but it was clear she loved

the sound of her own voice, the way she went on and on. I turned my head to Big Clay, my ears forward.

She says you'll be safe at our ranch, Big Clay said. *Her papa bought you from the men who captured you—ranchers that round up and kill wild mustangs, many as they can.*

Why kill us?

So their horses and sheep can have the range grasses to themselves.

But there was wild, wild grass all over the plains! There was plenty for all.

I don't believe you, I said. *They kill us because they're humans, predators, as bad as wolves and cougars. My mama told me that.*

Some of them ain't bad, Big Clay said.

Now who's a fool? I answered.

That Annie was just babbling on, and the sound of her voice hurt my ears, all talk and words that I didn't understand.

Clay turned away from me then and didn't tell me more of what she was saying. He just muttered, but loud enough for me to hear, *Stupid mustang. Real stupid. A know-it-all.*

That was what my mama had always said, too.

Still, I wasn't wrong, not about this. I knew predators when I met them. I hadn't forgotten the wolves. Or what the humans had done.

Annie kept on jabbering. Only a few of her words made sense. I knew *Mama* and I knew *horse* and *mustang,* mostly because of how she looked when she said those words.

After a while, Big Clay turned to me. *You got a name?* he asked.

Black Cloud.

He nickered then, maybe in approval, maybe in disapproval. I couldn't tell.

Annie turned to him. She slid from the fence, down onto his back again. She leaned forward, resting her head against his, and she ruffled up his ears and whispered to him.

He shook his head hard, making his ears flap.

Real grumpy-like, he spoke to me. *She won't hurt you.*

Will she turn me free? I asked.

Yes. On the ranch. Not out here on the plains. You'll get eaten by wolves. Cougars. We even got grizzlies up here.

I thought about that.

Annie kept on blabbering, her head still resting against Clay's neck and head. Clay threw in a word or two of what she was saying, but I had turned away from them both.

No, I didn't want to be alone out on the range. But I didn't want to be inside fences, either.

Something else, Big Clay said after a bit, still real grumpy-like, as if he really didn't want to tell me but he had to, maybe 'cause Annie told him to. *She talks a lot. Someday you'll understand. She wants to help.*

I didn't bother answering that. Trust her?

Annie was looking at me then, wondering-like. She took a deep breath, her eyes fixed on mine.

Big Clay was getting downright itchy, turning this way and that. "Whoa, boy, whoa!" she said, patting and comforting him, maybe urging him to keep on talking to me.

When she had him turned to face me, she started talking again. "Okay," she said. "I know you might not like staying with me, because you want to be free. We've rescued lots of wild mustangs, and they all want to be free."

Now I was listening. I knew the word *free*.

"Well," Annie went on, "I was once caged up, too. Last year, I had a bad disease, polio, and I had to live for a long time in a cage. And I couldn't move at all! So I know what it's like. But you *are* going to be able to run free. Only thing is, you can't run on the range alone. You know how wolves and cougars and coyotes will get you if you're alone. There are even bears up here. So you can run all over our ranch—it's huge—and come into the barns and corrals when it's cold or if you're scared, and you'll have a good home with me, and you'll be safe, too. The law says people can't hunt down mustangs on private lands."

All of this, Clay did tell me, just as I figured Annie had told him to. But he told me grudging-like. *You'll be safe with her,* he said. *You got a safe home.* He said it two, three times, like I was too stupid to understand.

I understood all right. But I didn't want a safe home, not with Clay, not with Annie. I already had a home. With Mama. On the range.

Only Mama was dead. And the herd was gone, dead, too. The only thing left was Clay, who wasn't any more free than I was, with a human stuck to his back. And a little girl who talked too much—and promised me something that I didn't want.

13

Still Not Free

I went in a thing called a truck, and I screamed and kicked and butted against it, but in a short time, a very short time, the humans opened it up. I bolted out into a large, open meadow.

It was the place Annie called the ranch.

With fences all around.

I ran from the humans that night, even though I was near to exhaustion. I flew off into a copse of trees, and there I stayed for a very long time. There was plenty of grazing and fresh-water, and so I stayed away from the humans, exploring, running as hard and far as I could. There were meadows and rocky slopes and spiky, spindly trees. There were little creeks, and birds that flew overhead. At night, the moon hung high in the sky, along with those stars that one day, long ago, I had thought I'd be able to touch. It was much like the wild range.

But there was no herd. There was no Mama to lead us. There were no family groups. There were no friends. There wasn't even mean old Sota, who had saved my life. There was no freedom. Because always—always—no matter how far or how fast I went, there were tall, tall fences. And something I recognized now as barbed wire.

I spent many moons roaming that place. The sun came up and went down. The moon came up, full and round, and then it turned and showed just a part of itself, just its edge, and then it turned round and fat again, and still I stayed away.

A few times, I went back to the place where I had first come into the ranch. There was a fence and a gate that looked to be made of trees. Men opened and closed that gate, coming in and out, on foot or on top of their horses. I plotted how to rush through when the gate opened. But I never got that chance. If the humans saw me close, they shouted and waved ropes at me, and I ran away, terrified.

Near the gate was a place Annie called the

corral. It was a big circle with its own fence around it. It was open on one end, though, so I could flee when I wanted. Inside the corral, Annie set out feed for me and water and some straw and hay where I could lie down, a place where I could sleep. After a while, I began to bed down inside that circle some nights.

It was awful lonely on the ranch with no

company. There were a few other mustangs running there, but none of them were from my family, not even my herd. They seemed as persnickety and distant as Big Clay, and I figured they didn't want to be there any more than I did. They just snorted and blew and ran around the edges of the ranch, away from me and one another, filled with the same frustration and fear that ate away at me.

I was really, really lonely. It got so that I was actually glad when Annie appeared near the corral—and she did that every single morning. If I was inside the corral, she sat herself atop the fence. And she talked to me. And talked. Each morning, she told me all the things she was doing to save the mustangs, and how she wrote letters to important people in the government. She told me that one of them was coming to visit and to listen to her.

I had begun to understand more of her language, especially because she combined her human talk with horse talk. Sometimes, she would look directly at me—never taking her eyes off me, her shoulders squared at me. It was just the way Mama did when teaching the youngsters in the herd. She was saying, *Go ahead, run away from me if you want. But I'll still be here when you come back.* I ran. And then she'd let her eyes slide back to my rump, and she was saying, *You can slow down now. I'm on your side; we're part of the same group.* Other times, even with her horse language, I didn't always understand. But I had begun to understand this: she was telling me we were on the same side.

So why wasn't she turning me free?

And then one morning, a man came with Annie. They both came atop horses, Annie riding Big Clay. They didn't come into the corral, but stayed on the far side of the fence.

"This is Senator Slattery," Annie called to me. "We rode out this morning, and I showed him where the mustangs were captured, and how those horrid men used the airplanes even though there's a law against doing that. Senator Slattery helped get that law passed. So now we're going to do even more. Mustangs can't be chased by planes on private lands. And we're fixing it so they can't be chased on public land, either. Ours is private, so you're good and safe, but you already know that. Someday soon, all mustangs will be safe. Wherever they are."

But I no longer believed in *safe*. I didn't care at all about laws or a man called senator, and I didn't know or care about public or private land. I wanted to be free. So when the man moved his horse a little closer to the fence, I reared and showed my teeth.

The man looked afraid, and soon he and Annie trotted away.

Before they left, though, Annie turned to me. "Now that," she said sternly, "was not very nice!"

Too bad, I thought.

Only thing was, I had begun to get used to Annie, even though she was human. I actually looked forward to her coming to the corral every day. Without the herd, I had no one to talk to at all, no one to listen to me, except for those persnickety horses who only wanted freedom, just as I did. And it seemed that they were too filled with their own misery to bother with me or even one another—though I noticed that some began to allow humans to touch them, and one—not just Clay—even allowed a human on his back! Were they the mustangs who had been around humans the longest? Or were they just the weak, docile ones, ones who had given in to loneliness, given up all hope of freedom?

And then, one morning, right after that senator person had come, instead of just sitting on the fence and talking, Annie jumped down inside the corral, standing close to me.

I reared up, then settled down.

Annie looked into my eyes. She didn't turn away, like that first time. She looked right at me, head to head, eye to eye. That was how Mama had looked when she'd forced Sota away.

Why?

I didn't know. But I turned and fled.

Annie followed me. On foot. She had nothing in her hands, nothing to capture me with. She just kept walking along, as though she were pushing me away from her.

I fled, running round and round, sticking close to the fence. Annie kept on walking behind, following me, facing me, her body turned to mine. And then that Annie stopped. She looked away. She turned away.

She walked away from me, as though she had no interest in making me run from her any longer. The game was over.

It was horse language she was using. I recognized it from my mama, from the mares. She was telling me that she could push me away—with her eyes, her body. But then she turned. And told me I could come back.

Well, I didn't want to go back. Instead, I bolted for the meadow.

Next day, though, I did go back. I was curious, just like my mama had always said I was. Again that day, Annie did the same thing. She walked toward me, and I ran from her. Then, after I had fled from her, she turned and went the other way.

This went on for many days.

And then, one day, when Annie turned to walk away, I followed.

I came up from behind. I got real close. She

stood still. She didn't turn to me. She didn't let her eyes slide sideways to look at me. She simply stood still. I came close, really close.

I touched her shoulder with my nose. She didn't move. She was as still as a rock, a tree.

Then she put a hand on my neck. I barely felt it. But it was there.

I fled.

14

A Strange Game

I stayed away for some days and nights. But after a while, I came back. And again, the same thing happened. Annie chased me away, then turned her back on me. Only now, I began to follow her. It was a game. But it was a game I liked.

I knew she was saying I could trust her. She

was safe. Not a predator. She would not harm me. We were partners. That was what the fleeing, then coming back, was telling me.

I began to like her voice, too, even though I didn't understand all of what she said, like about laws. Still, I knew she was telling me that she cared about me and about what happened to me. Not just me, but all mustangs.

After the day when I had fled from Annie's touch, she didn't touch me again for a long, long while. But then, one day, when I touched her with my nose, she once again put a hand on my neck. I could feel my flanks quiver, but I didn't flee. We stood together, until Annie moved away.

After that, each day, I let her stroke me more. And then, one day, she reached up to

scratch that place between my eyes. I let her do it. I was telling her that I trusted her. I did.

Strange, how I had begun to feel at home on the ranch. There were many other horses, ones like Big Clay, who let men ride on their backs, and mustangs like me, wild and still angry. But none of those mustangs went anywhere near Annie. I was the only one who trusted her, I guess. Was I a fool?

There were also other animals that I came to

know as bulls and sheep and cows. There were humans, too, but I kept away from them.

And then, one evening around sunset, Annie came to the corral to play our game. She walked toward me, and I ran away, round and round the corral. Annie stopped and turned away. I followed her, as always.

Only that evening, she did something different. When I came close, rather than just touch and scratch my head, she laid herself against me. She reached her arms over my back and stayed there awhile.

"There," she murmured. "There."

I leaned into her as she leaned into me. We stood that way. Together.

Me. And a human.

I hardly knew what to think.

15

A New Chance

Soon enough, winds began to howl, and the snows came, covering up the earth. The pickings were slim for grazing—though back in the corral, Annie always had grain and hay set out for me. Then, after a while, the snow slowly melted off the ridges and tiny shoots of green appeared.

And after that, the sun beat fiercely down upon us. Years were passing. I had been on the ranch for three years, Annie said, and I was a grown horse now. And I was still sad. Yes, I liked Annie. But I longed for freedom. I even wanted a mare, a family of my own.

I knew Annie knew of my sadness. One evening, when she came to the corral for our game, and we were chasing one another around, I suddenly stopped. The ground had moved lightly beneath my feet.

"What?" Annie asked.

The ground trembled some more.

"What is it?" Annie asked.

A herd. Running free.

"Something's worrying you," she said. "Do you want to stop our game?"

Yes.

My heart was pounding hard and even hurting a little.

Annie moved closer to me. "What is it?" she asked again. "Are you frightened?"

No. A herd. Far off, somewhere, a herd was traveling. I was sure of it. And from the way the ground moved, it was a huge herd.

Sounds began to reach us then, muffled, soft, like distant thunder. I trotted to the fence, leaning my neck way out, my ears pricked forward, my eyes fixed on the horizon. Night was coming, and a mist was rising over the range, and I peered through it.

Annie climbed up on the fence beside me. She looked toward the horizon also, and I heard her make a sound. She had seen it, too. Far away, far, far away, high along the ridge, a cloud of dust was rising. I couldn't yet see the mustangs. But they were there. I knew.

Could I get to them?

Did I want to?

Wild herds were hunted down. By humans with wings. And here, I was safe.

But I wasn't free.

The herds ran free.

Still, even if I joined up, wild herds didn't always welcome outsiders.

I was big now, though, almost a full-grown stallion. I could fight my way in if need be. I'd learned a lot since I was that scared little colt who feared Sota. Or I could stay around the edges till the herd got used to me and let me in.

For a really long time, I stood there watching, listening, Annie beside me. And then, through the mists and the rising dust, the herd came into view. I could make out shapes: stallions running along the outer edges of the herd, their tails high. Mares leading. And colts, many, many colts and fillies.

Closer they came, and closer. Manes were flying, and I could feel the thundering of hooves up close. I breathed in their familiar wild mustang smell.

There were different family groups, some with just a few mares, some with many, and it took a very long time for each one to pass. Then, once a group passed, another came on.

Annie slid closer to me along the fence. She

laid a hand on my head. She stroked that place
between my eyes. I leaned into her.

"Do you want to join them?" Annie whispered. "Do you want to run free?"

Did I?

For a long time, we continued to stand together, watching, listening. And then Annie climbed down from the fence. She left the corral. She went out to the swinging gate, the one that looked as though it was made of trees. She reached high and lifted the heavy crossbar that kept it closed. She pushed hard against it, and the gate swung wide.

I stared at that open gate, my heart thudding inside of me. I didn't move.

Annie came back. She climbed the fence beside me. It was dark now, and stars were just beginning to peep out. Annie put her hand on my head. I bent my neck and again leaned into her, letting her scratch that place between my eyes.

I backed away then, turned, and trotted to the gate. For a very long time, I stood by that open gate. A very long time.

And then I made my decision.

APPENDIX

MORE ABOUT THE MUSTANG

Early History

It is widely believed that most horses in the United States today are descendants of horses brought here by the Spanish colonists. The horse actually originated in North America, having lived here for over fifty million years. Then, about eight to ten thousand years ago, for reasons that are not fully understood, the horse in North America became extinct.

Horses were reintroduced when the Spanish colonists came to America in the 1400s and 1500s, bringing with them some of their finest horses. These horses were mated, and their populations grew. Once the native peoples of North America, as well as military and others, saw how useful horses were, the supply was not big enough to meet the demand. Breeding farms were set up, providing a rich supply of horses, many of whom later roamed freely. These free-roaming mustangs (named after the Spanish word *mesteño*, which means *wild* or *stray*), although many people call them wild, are technically feral, which means that their ancestors were domesticated.

Since they come from widely mixed backgrounds, mustangs vary in coat colors. They can be brown or black or white, or combinations of colors. They also vary in size. Horses are measured in "hands"—a hand being about four inches. The measurement is taken at the withers, an area by the shoulder blades. Thus, sixteen hands is a little over five feet tall. Most mustangs stand about thirteen hands tall, but some can be as tall as sixteen hands.

Overpopulation

Unfortunately, mustangs were so well suited to their new home that their success at breeding

was also their downfall. During the early part of
the twentieth century, an estimated two million
mustangs roamed over the range lands in the
West, many of them in Nevada. Instead of
people viewing them as potentially useful as
well as beautiful, there was great pressure to "do

something" to control the herds. The mustangs were competing with domesticated livestock for grazing land and water rights.

The horror of trapping and killing and even torturing these wild mustangs began. Ranchers took part in systematic killings, rounding up mustang herds by plane or helicopter or with land vehicles. The mustangs were corralled, then sent off to slaughterhouses. The meat was sold as dog food, or sometimes shipped overseas to countries that permitted the sale of horse meat for human consumption. The ranchers claimed nothing else could be done to maintain the land for their livestock.

Others, however, thought differently.

Wild Horse Annie

As awareness of the mustangs' situation came to the public eye, the horror began to change. Many of these changes were due to the actions of a woman named Velma Bronn Johnston, nicknamed Wild Horse Annie. The real Wild Horse Annie was a grown woman at the time *Black Cloud* takes place. Annie had a great affinity for horses, having grown up with them on a ranch where horses were treated with respect and dignity. She had been confined to a breathing apparatus for a long year as a child, possibly due to polio, and she keenly understood the need to be free. She had also seen up close the cruelty that was now being perpetrated on mustangs in the wild. Thus, she began a campaign to bring public attention to the plight of the horses. One of the many ways she did this was by enlisting the help of schoolchildren, asking them to bring their concerns to the attention of their senators and representatives.

Thousands of letters written by young people

Wild Horse Annie showed these photographs of cruelty to mustangs to Congress in 1959.

from all over the country poured into officials' offices, begging them to protect the horses. Children even sent small amounts of money to help in the effort. Annie, along with Nevada state senator James Slattery, was able to get laws passed that prevented the roundup and slaughter of mustangs on private lands in Nevada. However, since so much of the state was open land, that law had very little effect.

Annie didn't give up. With speeches to Congress and to any public audience willing to listen, and with the perseverance of the children, Annie was able to have another, more effective law passed in 1959, which became known as the Wild Horse Annie Act. This act ensured that wild horses could no longer be hunted and captured on private *or* state land.

Still, this was not enough for Wild Horse Annie. She continued her work on behalf of the horses, and in 1971, Congress unanimously passed the Wild Free-Roaming Horse and Burro Act, which was signed into law by President Nixon on December 15, 1971. This act made it illegal to capture or disturb any free-roaming horse. The act also mandated that horses be transferred if the land where they lived could no longer sustain them. Mustangs now roam free in protected sanctuaries—many of them in Nevada.

However, as helpful and humane as these acts were, there is still a problem: what is to be done about the many horses who continue to proliferate in the Western lands as well as in the sanctuaries? In some places, the land has been stripped of vegetation and the environment cannot support these horses.

Today, there are dozens of organizations that support the humane management of these animals, within the parameters of the congressional acts. There are events throughout the country that let people adopt mustangs—though the adoption process and the keeping and training of mustangs are not easy. There are also organizations dedicated to finding ways to control the mustang population and to locating places for the horses to live and thrive.

Much gratitude is due to Wild Horse Annie, as well as to the children who helped her. They succeeded in protecting the lives of the mustangs and the land on which they live.

⇐ COMING SOON! ⇐

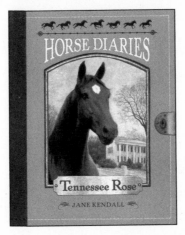

Alabama, 1856

Tennessee Rose is a dark bay Tennessee Walking Horse with a rose-shaped mark on her forehead. She loves dashing around the plantation in the running walk that her breed is famous for, then coming back to her stall and her friend Levi, the slave boy who is her groom. But as the Civil War approaches, Rosie begins to question slavery, and to hope that Levi will be free. Here is Rosie's story . . . in her own words.

About the Author

Patricia Hermes is the author of over forty novels for children and young adults and two nonfiction books for adults.

As a child, she fell in love with horses and spent many a day (and night) "stealing" rides bareback on a neighbor horse who grazed in a nearby field. However, since she grew up in and around New York City, and since horseback riding was an expensive proposition, there weren't many opportunities for lessons. Later, though, when she got older and moved, there was much more opportunity to connect with her beloved horses, especially in places like Virginia and Connecticut. She no longer had to "steal" rides, but began taking riding lessons, and was particularly attracted to—and challenged by—a classically beautiful type of riding called dressage, also sometimes called horse ballet. Although she has never "owned" a horse, many horses have owned her heart.

A resident of Connecticut, and the mother of five, she frequently speaks at schools and conferences around the country.

About the Illustrators

When **Astrid Sheckels** was growing up, she was never happier than when she had a paintbrush or pencil in her hand, a good book to read, and a furry animal nearby. Her favorite things to draw were animals, both real and imaginary.

Astrid is a fine artist and the illustrator of a number of picture books and novels, including the award-winning *The Scallop Christmas* and *The Fish House Door*. She still likes to sneak animals into her illustrations! She lives and maintains her studio in the rolling hills of Western Massachusetts.

To learn more about Astrid and her work, visit astridsheckels.com.

Ruth Sanderson grew up with a love for horses. She has illustrated and retold many fairy tales and likes to feature horses in them whenever possible. Her book about a magical horse, *The Golden Mare, the Firebird, and the Magic Ring,* won the Texas Bluebonnet Award.

Ruth and her daughter have two horses, an Appaloosa named Thor and a quarter horse named Gabriel. She lives with her family in Massachusetts.

To find out more about her adventures with horses and the research she does to create Horse Diaries illustrations, visit her website, ruthsanderson.com.

Collect all the books in the
Horse Diaries series!

Elska

CATHERINE HAPKA

Illustrated by RUTH SANDERSON

Bell's Star

ALISON HART

Illustrated by RUTH SANDERSON

Koda

PATRICIA HERMES

Illustrated by RUTH SANDERSON

Maestoso Petra

JANE KENDALL

Illustrated by RUTH SANDERSON

Golden Sun

WHITNEY SANDERSON

Illustrated by RUTH SANDERSON

Yatimah

CATHERINE HAPKA

Illustrated by RUTH SANDERSON

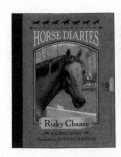

And coming soon!